**READER BEWARE —
DO NOT READ THIS
BOOK FROM
BEGINNING TO END!**

The new multiplex is finally open — and you're first in line to see one of three killer movies.

What will it be? Choose *Going Ape in Blastovision* or *House of a Hundred Horrors*, and you'll get a big shock — when you get sucked right into the big screen! Before you escape, you'll have to face ferocious giant apes, cannibals, and even vampires. But don't think you're taking the easy way out if you choose *Agent Z vs. Dr. Aqua*. Just one warning: Look out for humanigators!

This scary adventure is all about *you*. You decide what will happen. And you decide how terrifying the scares will be!

Start on Page 1. Then follow the instructions at the bottom of each page. You make the choices. If you choose well, you'll live through your big-screen adventure. But if you make the wrong choice . . . BEWARE!

SO TAKE A DEEP BREATH. CROSS YOUR FINGERS. AND TURN TO PAGE 1 TO *GIVE YOURSELF GOOSEBUMPS!*

READER BEWARE —
YOU CHOOSE THE SCARE!

Look for more
GIVE YOURSELF GOOSEBUMPS adventures
from R.L. STINE:

R.L. STINE

GIVE YOURSELF

Goosebumps®

INVADERS FROM
THE BIG SCREEN

AN
APPLE
PAPERBACK

SCHOLASTIC INC.
New York Toronto London Auckland Sydney

A PARACHUTE PRESS BOOK

ISBN 0-590-40289-7

12 11 10 9 8 7 6 5 4 3 2 1   8 9/9 0 1 2 3/0

Printed in the U.S.A.   40

First Scholastic printing, July 1998

"Finally!" You step up to the ticket window. You feel as if you and your friend Laura have been standing in line at the multiplex all day! As usual, you spent the entire time arguing about which movie to see.

Laura is nervous about seeing *House of a Hundred Horrors*. She's kind of a movie wimp. *Going Ape in Blastovision* is another possibility. A movie about a giant ape trained for combat games could be cool. Especially since the ads promise that Blastovision makes you feel as if you're *in* the movie.

But watching your favorite superhero, Agent Z, battling the evil villain, Dr. Aqua, might be a good choice too.

"So what will it be?" the woman behind the window asks.

You turn to Laura. "Okay," you announce. "Time's up. We have to choose."

Laura rolls her eyes. "You pick," she declares. "You always hate the movies I like anyway."

That's just what you hoped she would say. . . . But now it's up to you.

To see House of a Hundred Horrors, *turn to PAGE 120.*

To see Agent Z vs. Dr. Aqua, *turn to PAGE 9.*

For Going Ape in Blastovision, *turn to PAGE 84.*

"Okay," you declare. "We'll help you find Aunt Kitty."

"And we'll help you find your way back to the movie theater," John promises.

You follow the twins down a long, dark hallway lined with life-size paintings of sad, weird-looking people. Cobwebs cling to the frames. You shudder, wondering if these people fell into this house like you and never got out.

You arrive at a crumbling staircase leading down. "Do you know where that goes?" you ask the twins.

Before they can answer, you hear a noise behind you.

"What's that?" you cry, whirling around. Then you laugh. The sound that scared you is just the *THWUMP, THWUMP, THWUMP* of a large bouncing ball. You're about to make a joke when you realize there *is* something terrifying about that ball.

No one is bouncing it!

Laura drags you to the staircase. "Let's go," she urges. "Before that bouncing ball bounces over here."

But maybe you should try to catch the ball. Find out where it came from.

Or maybe you should stick with the plan to find Aunt Kitty. . . .

Catch the ball on PAGE 121.
Run down the stairs on PAGE 46.

Hours pass. Still no ape.

"I guess this perfume isn't so irresistible after all," you comment.

You hear the hunter pacing above you. "I must not have used enough," he mutters.

"Whoa! Yeccchhh!"

A vat of the stinky perfume pours down on you. As you wipe the slimy stuff out of your eyes the ground shakes and rumbles.

"Is it an earthquake?" Laura screams.

You strain to reach the top of the pit. You peer over the edge. And gasp.

"Stampede!" you shriek. "All the animals in the jungle are heading this way!"

The hunter was right. The perfume is irresistible. The kind of scent that really knocks 'em dead.

The wearer, that is . . .

THE END

4

"Are you serious?" you demand. "We escaped from that monster once. There's no guarantee that we'll escape twice!"

"But I guarantee it!" The hunter smiles broadly at you. "I'm the greatest hunter who ever lived!"

"We only have *your* word for that," Laura retorts. She tugs your arm. "Let's get out of here."

"I wouldn't go anywhere if I were you," the hunter warns. "This jungle is filled with dangerous creatures."

You glance at Laura. He might have a point. He just saved you from that poisonous spider. Who knows what else lurks in the thick vegetation?

"Don't trust him," Laura whispers. "He gives me the creeps."

Do you try to find your way home on your own? Turn to PAGE 107.

Or agree to act as bait on PAGE 70.

This is so cool! You've always wanted to be a superagent like Agent Z. And his world is full of neat gadgets and high-tech stuff.

Agent Z pulls two pairs of flippers from his backpack and tosses them to you and Laura. "Put those on," he instructs you.

You do as he says. "I'm not a great swimmer," you confess. "I don't know how long I'll be able to keep up."

"Don't worry, kid," Agent Z assures you. "The Flying Flippers will do all the work. Just pull the activation cord — and don't let go. You'll need to pull it again to stop."

You and Laura wrap the long blue cords around your wrists. You give yours a sharp tug. The flippers propel you forward.

"Whoa!" you exclaim. "Awesome!" The Flying Flippers are motorized! You skim easily across the top of the water.

"It's like waterskiing without the water skis!" Laura shouts over the motors.

"Follow me! And be prepared for anything," Agent Z calls.

You heard the guy. Follow him to PAGE 18.

You glance around for something heavy enough to damage the security system. You find a strange-looking chair. "Look — there's a tail hole! I guess it's designed for humanigators," you figure.

You raise the chair over your head. You bring it down hard on the console.

CRASH!

You wait to hear some kind of alarm or sirens. Nothing. Nothing but a strange whooshing sound. Then all the electronic gadgets and pumps and valves start going into high gear.

Laura dashes to a porthole. "We're moving!" she cries. "That console wasn't just a security system. It controls *everything*."

Uh-oh.

Turn to PAGE 54.

As your eyes adjust to the darkness you discover something strange. The theater is empty!

"Great choice," Laura taunts you. "This movie must be so bad they probably would have paid *us* to see it!"

"Or maybe it's so scary everyone is too afraid to come," you tease. You know Laura gets nervous at scary movies.

"I guess we'll find out," she replies, settling into a seat.

You sit beside her. The lights dim. Music begins. The opening credits flicker across the screen.

THWACK! WHAP!

"Huh?" You feel a sharp slap against your stomach. You glance down.

A seatbelt has snapped around your waist!

You tug at it. It's locked tight.

Laura yanks her seatbelt too. "I guess they automatically buckle at the beginning of the movie," she suggests.

"I just hope they automatically *un*buckle at the end," you joke. "But why would we need seatbelts to watch a movie?"

Good question.

Find out the answer on PAGE 40.

"What could be dangerous about a musical interlude?" you say. You enter the room and discover a large grand piano.

Playing itself.

"No big deal," you declare. "I've seen player pianos before."

"Not like this one." Laura points to the keyboard.

She's right. Instead of black and white keys, this piano has black and white *teeth*!

"Check this out," John calls. He stands by a row of doors numbered 1 through 5.

"And this!" Wendy holds up a piece of sheet music. "I bet it's some kind of clue."

"How can it be a clue?" you argue. "It's just musical notes."

"You're the one who took piano lessons," Laura responds. "You figure it out."

You study the music carefully. "I think the notes spell out a word," you suggest. "If we play them correctly."

Laura nods at the piano. "Go to it, maestro."

If only you practiced more . . .

Go to PAGE 99 for your clue.

"I can't wait to see what terrible plot Dr. Aqua comes up with this time!" You settle into your seats as the movie begins.

"And how Agent Z defeats him!" Laura agrees.

VRRRRROOOMMM! Dr. Aqua roars into view on his supercharged Jet Ski. His webbed fingers expertly handle the controls. His gills flap in the strong wind.

"Soon all my dreams will come true," the fish-like scientist declares. "I shall flood the entire world!"

"Not if I can stop you!" a voice cries.

"Agent Z!" you and Laura cheer.

Agent Z is at the helm of a sleek blue powerboat. He wears a slick wet suit. He presses some buttons on the control panel. The boat hovers several inches above the water! It zooms after Dr. Aqua.

"Eat my spray!" Dr. Aqua hollers before shifting into high gear. The pair make so many dizzying maneuvers you feel seasick. Finally Dr. Aqua reaches a giant dam.

"There's no escape!" Agent Z calls. "Give up now!"

"Fat chance," you mutter. "If he surrenders, the movie is over."

You're right! So find out what happens on PAGE 102.

Laura tugs your arm so sharply you cry out. "Hey! What?"

Then you realize. You were heading straight into the net!

You would have been trapped with the gorilla!

You and Laura peel off, never for a moment relaxing your pace. You keep running. And running. Your head throbs with the pounding of your blood. Sweat pours down your face, your neck, your back.

CRASHHHHH!

The thunderous crash makes you stop. You turn to see what has happened. Dozens of toppled trees block your view. But then you hear cheering.

"It worked," Laura pants. "They must have captured the giant ape."

You nod. You don't have enough breath to speak.

Turn to PAGE 47.

You started this. Now you're going to finish it!

"Hey, you dumb ape, this way!" You jump up and down, trying to attract his attention.

"We've got to get past him so that we can lead him into those nets," Laura whispers.

But how do you get past the ape without being grabbed?

BOOM! BOOM! The ape takes thundering steps toward you.

"He can't move very fast," you point out. "Why don't we wait until he gets up close, then dash through his legs? We just have to make sure to stay out of reach."

"Piece of cake," Laura mutters sarcastically.

"Do you have a better idea?" you demand.

"I think we should run around him in different directions," Laura says. "He won't know which way to look."

"If we split up, it'll be easier to catch us," you argue.

"Or more confusing," Laura suggests.

You've agreed to play chicken with the gorilla. Now all you need to decide is what route to take into the trap.

If you run between his legs, turn to PAGE 20.
If you split up and run around each side, turn to PAGE 100.

You scramble out of the net so fast it tips over. Laura falls to the ground.

"Thanks a lot," she mutters. She wipes dirt off her shorts as she scrambles to her feet.

A fat man wearing khaki shorts and shirt emerges from the bushes. His white pith helmet reflects the bright sun. You have to squint to see him. A thick mustache with curled ends covers his upper lip. A rifle is strapped across his back. He carries a long black whip.

"Hi!" you greet him. This must be the hunter in the movie. "We were hoping to run into you."

But the man doesn't answer. He stares at you so intently you feel as if he can see straight through to the tree behind you. You don't like the way he's uncoiling the whip.

"Uh, listen," you begin again.

WHAP! With a sharp snap of the wrist, the hunter flicks the whip at you!

Jump back on PAGE 110.

You stare at the terrifying mutants. They have long, powerful tails and alligator snouts with large, sharp teeth.

You jump when one of them snaps his jaws at you. The other lifts a scaly hand in salute.

You let out a deep sigh of relief. They actually think you're one of them. The costume is working!

You nod sharply. Then you try to keep your legs from trembling as you walk by them.

You feel their lidless eyes follow you.

"You there," one of them calls. "Turn around. Slowly."

Do what he says. Turn to PAGE 78.

14

"Run!" you order. "Those humanigators could be here any minute!"

You and Laura dash down the corridor. Agent Z told you how many turns to take to get to the lab. "One. Two. Three," you count under your breath. You skid to a stop. "Here."

You stand in front of a door marked LABORA-TORY. Laura nods. You throw open the door. Your mouth drops open in shock.

The whole room is like a swamp. Your feet sink into mucky, muddy water. Tall plants grow out of the floor. Drooping trees hang overhead. The steamy air stinks.

"Alligator paradise," Laura murmurs.

"Where are the machines? The equipment?" You scan the room. You notice a metallic glint just beyond a clump of cattails.

You and Laura slog through the thick, gooey mud. You brush aside the overgrown plants. You stare at a row of knobs and buttons. The control panel is labeled . . .

"Flooding Device!" you cry. "We found it!"

A snarl behind you makes you whirl around.

"What are you doing in here?" a humanigator demands from the doorway.

Turn to PAGE 35.

You dash to a stone archway. You peek out to try to discover what is making that awful noise.

"Weird," you murmur. A suit of armor clanks down the hall. You turn back to the twins. "Uh, guys? Any reason a knight in armor would be roaming around down here?"

Laura snickers. "Do you think Aunt Kitty is dressed up in a knight suit?"

"D-d-did you say armor?" John stammers.

You don't like how scared he sounds. Or how pale his face is suddenly.

"We've heard terrible stories," Wendy wails from the corner. "About empty suits of armor searching for a body."

Empty? How can an empty suit of armor get around? you wonder.

"We don't know it's empty," you point out. You peek out from the archway again. Laura squeezes beside you.

The knight stands in the hallway. Slowly, he turns his head. You figure he's trying to decide which way to go.

Then you notice his visor is up.

And instead of a face — there's nothing!

Turn to PAGE 83.

Gazing around, you realize that the room isn't completely empty. A large dresser stands against the far wall.

"Let's check it out." You all cross to the dresser. There's lettering on the middle drawer. You wipe away the dirt and read the words aloud.

"'Helter-Skelter Drawer. If at first you don't succeed, try, try again.'" You gaze up at Laura and the twins. "What do you think the message means?"

Laura shrugs. "Leave it alone. Everything in this place is too weird."

But you can't resist. You slowly pull open the drawer. You fumble around until you feel something smooth. You wrap your fingers around it and pull it out.

"A key!" Laura exclaims. She takes it from you.

"Maybe it's the key to where Aunt Kitty is," John suggests. "Check the drawer again."

"No," Laura objects. "We should keep searching for Aunt Kitty. I think that armor has given up on us."

"We might find something else we'll need," Wendy argues.

"Or something deadly," Laura counters.

All three of them stare at you. What should you do?

If you reach into the drawer again, turn to PAGE 108.

If you leave the room, go to PAGE 45.

The ape's enormous body fills the screen. You find yourself pushing hard against the back of your seat. The image is so lifelike you want to put some distance between you and the ape.

The gorilla beats its massive chest with huge fists. It throws back its head and lets out a deafening cry.

"Aahhh!" Laura shrieks and covers her ears.

The ape grabs a nearby tree trunk and tosses it to the ground. The impact jerks you hard in your seat.

"I never thought you could get whiplash at the movies!" you exclaim. You notice Laura has turned pale beside you.

BOOM! BOOM! ROOOAR! The ape jumps up and down, letting out enraged cries. The walls of the movie theater shudder. Lights crash to the ground. The noise is horrendous.

Your seats shake so violently the seatbelts snap open. You can hear the bolts in your chairs squeaking — ready to fly apart.

"There must be something wrong with the Blastovision!" Laura cries. "Let's get out of here!"

To stay for the rest of the movie, turn to PAGE 115.

To leave, go to PAGE 60.

Agent Z leads you to a boat anchored near Dr. Aqua's underwater fortress. You can't believe all the amazing gadgets and gizmos he has.

"Whoa," you exclaim. "Does all this stuff really work? Or are they just movie props?" You reach for a speargun.

"Watch it, kid," Agent Z snaps. "This world is just as real as yours. And just as dangerous. Make that *more* dangerous."

You gulp. And leave the speargun on its shelf.

Agent Z explains his plan as he equips you with scuba gear. "We'll break into Dr. Aqua's underwater fortress and destroy the flooding devices."

You and Laura suit up. "Do you think we'll run into any humanigators?" Laura asks nervously.

You remember Dr. Aqua's humanigators from the preview. They are half-human, half-alligator mutants created by the evil scientist to carry out his latest plot. You shudder just thinking about them.

"Count on it," Agent Z answers.

Turn to PAGE 42.

"Shush!" The hunter comes to such a sudden stop, you and Laura bang into him. "Get down."

You and Laura duck under a low palm tree. You watch the hunter peering through the thick foliage. "There he is," the hunter whispers.

"Where?" Laura tries to stand to look, but you yank her back down.

The hunter sends up a flare. "Now my mates will know the beast has been spotted — and where," he explains. "They'll get the nets ready."

You and Laura sit hunched under the palm tree waiting for the hunter to receive the return signal.

"They're ready!" he cries. "Now go get that gorilla!"

Dash over to PAGE 27.

"We should stick together," you insist. "When he gets close enough, we'll run between his legs straight toward the nets."

"Just remember not to run *into* them," Laura cautions.

The ape lashes out one of his powerful arms. You and Laura leap out of reach.

BOOM! He takes another step toward you. He tries again. And fails.

He throws back his head and roars in frustration.

"Now!" you scream. "While he's not looking down!"

You and Laura race toward the ape. He glances down and spots you below him. But as he stretches his huge palm toward you, you dash between his feet.

His own body protects you from his grasp. But you don't stop. You and Laura keep running. Your heart pounds with fear and effort. You hear Laura panting beside you. The nets. You can see the nets straight ahead.

BOOM! BOOM!

"Is he following us?" you shout to the hunters holding the nets. "Is the plan working?"

The ape's deafening cry drowns out the answer.

Turn to PAGE 10.

Before Laura can answer, you are startled by a large flash. A moment later the lights flick back on.

"Agent Z!" you cry.

The superagent stands over the humanigator. "These laser pens come in handy," he comments. Then he helps you and Laura down. "Great job, kids. The world is safe again."

You and Laura grin. You feel very proud.

"As a thank-you gift, I want you to have these." He hands you each a pair of sunglasses. Just like the trademark shades he always wears.

"Thanks!" You put on the glasses.

Instantly, you find yourself back in the movie theater, staring at the screen. The words THE END flicker and fade.

"Wow," you murmur. "Did that really happen?"

Laura taps her pair of Agent Z sunglasses. "You bet!"

"We really did it!" you exclaim. "We stopped Dr. Aqua!" You're glad Laura was part of this adventure. Otherwise you would never believe it was true!

You and Laura leave the theater. You wish you could tell everyone that you and Laura met Agent Z and saved the world.

But who would believe you?

So you somehow keep this secret to the very

END.

You brace yourself for the sharp metal spikes.

Nothing! Instead of piercing pain, you feel a cool breeze coming from above you.

That means there's an opening somewhere overhead!

You feel around carefully in the blackness. You don't want to get spiked! What you discover is that the iron maiden is built into the wall. The opening you crawled into is the foot of a narrow staircase.

"Come on," you call. "The parrot was right. This *does* lead upstairs!"

The four of you carefully make your way up the tiny, winding staircase. At the top is a trapdoor. You climb out and find yourselves in a dusty hall-way lined with tall wooden doors.

You dash over to the first door and turn the knob. Locked.

Laura and the twins try opening doors.

They're all locked.

Turn to PAGE 23.

"Great," John grumbles. "Aunt Kitty could be behind any one of those doors, and we can't get to her."

"Maybe we can," Laura pipes up. She pulls a key out of her pocket. The key from the Helter-Skelter Drawer.

"But which door?" Wendy asks. "There are dozens of them."

You scan the hallway. You point to three doors at the end. "Those are the only doors that take an old-fashioned key like this one," you state.

"Great! That narrows it down," Laura says. "But which one should we try first?"

You approach the doors with the old-fashioned locks. A large sign hangs above them. You gulp as you read it out loud: "'Behind these doors, danger lurks.'"

You notice each door has a faint inscription. One door reads PLAYTIME. The middle door reads MUSICAL INTERLUDE. The last door reads PORTRAITS.

Hmmm. They don't sound very scary.

Laura holds the key out to you. "Which door should we try?"

If you open the door that reads PLAYTIME, *turn to* PAGE 131.

If you try MUSICAL INTERLUDE, *turn to* PAGE 8. *For* PORTRAITS, *turn to* PAGE 31.

24

"No way am I getting into that thing. Especially not on the advice of a parrot!" You slam the back panel shut again. "Let's keep looking."

You all head back out into the stone corridor.

And walk right into the empty suit of armor.

"Oh, no!" you gasp. You take a step backward and stumble into Laura. She trips and crashes into the twins. The four of you land in a heap on the cold stone floor.

"Bodies," the suit of armor announces hollowly. "The bodies I have been seeking."

"No way, metal-head!" You leap up and shove the suit of armor as hard as you can. It clatters to the floor. As it struggles to stand, you, Laura, and the twins dash back into the room with the iron maiden.

You hear the suit of armor clanking down the hallway. It must have managed to stand back up.

No time to lose. You yank open the door on the side of the coffinlike box and dive into the iron maiden.

Turn to PAGE 22.

"Aunt Kitty! Aunt Kitty!" the twins wail. Then they also shriek in pain and fall to the floor. The vampire bats must have attacked them also.

As your vision dims you see the face of an old woman over you. "Aunt Kitty! Get out quick! Before the vampires get you."

But the woman just smiles at you. Then she laughs. That's when you notice her teeth. *Her fangs.*

Oh, no. Now you understand why Aunt Kitty was locked in the tower. She's a deadly vampire. And now you've let her go. To attack more innocent people.

And you're a vampire too! What's worse — you're a *movie* vampire. Which means from now on you have to wear a ratty old cape, have stupid-looking, shiny black helmet hair, and talk with a totally fake accent.

THE END

"Okay, start hunting!" you cry. You and Laura race around the laundromat, trying to figure out how to shut off the washers.

Laura unplugs them — but they still keep flooding.

You slam down their lids — but they burst open again.

Then you follow a row of pipes that intersect down near the floor. "I think I found the valve!" you cry.

Good for you! You found the valve that controls the main water supply.

The only problem is, you turn it the wrong way!

With the increased water pressure, the washing machines explode. If the flying debris doesn't get you, the rising water will.

Oh, well. Looks like you're all washed up!

THE END

"Go! Go!" the hunter cries. He shoves you so hard that you're sent sprawling on the ground.

Laura helps you to your feet. "Move it!" the hunter screams furiously.

You move it.

The ape is only yards away from you. But his back is turned, so he hasn't seen you yet.

You peer into the jungle. You can just make out the hunters holding the huge nets in place.

Laura tugs your arm. "Maybe we should forget capturing the ape. Maybe we should make a run for it."

The ape must have heard her. He turns around and glares at you.

"ROOOAAAARRRRRRR!"

Gulp.

It's now or never. Either start playing cat and mouse with the gorilla, or try to make a break for it.

To run away, turn to PAGE 76.
To lure the ape into the trap, turn to PAGE 11.

"If getting upstairs is what you like," the parrot repeats, "climb in the box but avoid the spikes."

You stare at the iron maiden. "Get in *there*?" you exclaim.

"Get in there? Get in there?" The parrot mocks you.

"You're crazy!" you shout at the parrot. "I'm not getting in that thing."

"You're crazy! You're crazy!" the parrot squawks.

"Wait," Laura interrupts. "Maybe there's another way to get inside the iron maiden."

You stop yelling at the parrot and stare at the iron maiden. The four of you examine the deadly box. You discover a small handle on the side. You yank it open.

All you see is black.

"Should we get in?" Laura asks shakily.

Your palms sweat as you think about the sharp metal spikes. Either the iron maiden will be the way upstairs — or it will turn you into a big piece of Swiss cheese.

What should you do?

If you climb into the iron maiden, turn to PAGE 22.

If you keep searching for a way upstairs, turn to PAGE 24.

Your heart pounds double time. *Dozens* of alligators swim toward you.

You and Laura splash to shore. You hope to lose them in the brush. They won't be able to climb over all the twisted branches and thick roots.

But, to your horror, the alligators follow you onto land.

Then they rise up on two legs and chase you!

"They're not alligators!" Laura shrieks. "They're mutants."

You remember seeing horrible creatures like this. In the commercial for the new Agent Z movie! They're terrible half-man, half-alligator mutants called *humanigators*.

Following the river was supposed to bring you closer to home. Instead, you somehow wound up in the preview for *Agent Z vs. Dr. Aqua!*

Well, you and Laura are the first kids on your block to see the humanigators. From the inside out!

THE END

"Do I look like Tarzan?" you demand. "We're *climbing* down."

The ape's palm rests on top of a large tree. The tree's huge leaves are broad enough for you and Laura to scramble onto.

"Whoa!" you cry. The leaf is strong, but it bends under your weight. "Quick! Grab onto the trunk."

You clutch the thick trunk and slide toward it. Carefully, you dangle your foot below to the next branch. You ease yourself down. Laura follows behind you.

Slowly, very slowly, you make your way toward the ground.

CRAAACKK! "Nooo!" you shriek as the branch you and Laura hang from snaps and breaks. You plunge down. You're about to hit the ground with a bone-crushing thud.

But instead, you land in a rope net strung between the bottom branches. You and Laura bounce a few times before coming to a stop.

You shake your head, trying to clear it. You try to grasp everything that has happened. Somehow, you wound up in the movie. Now how are you going to get back to reality? Alive!

Before you can discuss the problem with Laura, you hear crackling in the underbrush.

Turn to PAGE 12.

You enter a room filled with portraits. Just like the ones in the hallway. But these paintings are only half-finished. Some are missing hands, noses, ears. And they all look twisted and misshapen. You notice a particularly gruesome one is missing his eyes.

"These paintings are creepy," Laura comments.

She's right. You hate how it feels as if they're all watching you. Except for the painting in front of you. The one with no eyes.

"Beware!" a voice warns you. "Beware of the vampires!"

You scan the room. "Who said that?" you demand.

Laura grips your arm. She points a shaking finger at the eyeless portrait in front of you.

"He did," she whispers in terror. "The man in the painting."

Turn to PAGE 67.

32

The moment you sit at the piano bench, the piano stops playing. The sudden silence makes you nervous. Your fingers tremble as you place them on the toothy keyboard.

You play the notes slowly: F-A-D-E-D-A-G-E.

You remove your fingers quickly after the last note.

Silence.

More silence.

You are about to try again when the piano begins playing a new tune.

It sounds familiar. . . .

"I know that piece of music," Laura cries. "It's Beethoven's Fifth Symphony!"

You snort. "Big deal. How is that going to help us?"

Laura rushes over to the doors. "Don't you see? It must mean that Aunt Kitty is behind Door Number Five!"

"Brilliant," Wendy exclaims.

"Way to go," John adds.

You wish *you* had figured that out!

Use the key to open Door Number 5 on PAGE 105.

Laura's right, you decide. This is no time for fun and games. Right now the most important thing to do is find Aunt Kitty.

Your head whips up when you hear music playing in the next room. It sounds like a piano.

Who is in there? you wonder. Could it be Aunt Kitty? Or someone else who can help you?

Better go check it out.

Follow the music to PAGE 8.

You and Laura explain your situation to the ape. You ask him to help you find your way back to your own reality.

"Of course I will!" the gorilla promises. "I have just the thing."

In a few swift strides, the ape carries you back to where you entered the movie. He reaches into a hole in a tree and pulls out —

"The 3-D glasses!" you cry.

"I noticed you dropped them," the ape explains. "I thought you might need them, so I hid them in the tree for safekeeping."

"I'm sure the glasses are the key to getting home!" Laura exclaims. "Thank you."

The ape lowers you and Laura carefully to the ground. You and Laura are about to put on the glasses when the gorilla shouts, "Wait!"

Wait until PAGE 63.

"Quick!" Laura screams. "Do something!"

You and Laura push, click, turn, and flick every knob on the control panel. The machine goes berserk — lights flash, buzzers buzz, and finally it shorts out in a shower of sparks.

The lights go out.

"The humanigator!" you yell. "Where is it?"

"I don't know," Laura moans.

You grab her hand and drag her on top of the Flooding Device. You perch on top of the narrow machine. You peer down, trying to see the humanigator.

You notice a tiny light moving in the darkness. "What is that?" you whisper. "Another humanigator?"

Turn to PAGE 21.

36

"I'll take my chances with the cannibals," you retort. "It sounds a lot safer!"

Besides, you figure, maybe they've already had dinner.

You and Laura hurry off. Soon you come to a clearing. In the center roars a crackling fire. You shudder when you spot the large black cauldron suspended over the flames.

It's just your size!

You and Laura glance around. The place seems deserted. Where are the cannibals?

You cautiously head for the fire.

"Who are you?" a gruff voice behind you demands.

You whirl around and stare into a very mean, very ugly face.

Turn to PAGE 92.

You snap your fingers. "I know! Find a painting of a man wearing a hat with a tassel," you order. "That's where the key is hidden."

You scan the walls of the hallway. Unfortunately, most of the paintings are of men wearing hats. You, Laura, and the twins split up, searching for the right portrait.

Then you spot him — at the end of the hall. A painting of a tall man with a long black beard. Wearing a black hat with a tassel.

"There he is!" you exclaim. You all dash toward the painting. Laura and the twins crowd around you as you slowly remove the painting from the wall.

And are immediately plunged through the floor.

"It was the wrong painting!" Wendy cries.

"It triggered a trapdoor," John adds.

"No kidding," you mutter. As you plummet through the darkness, you make yourself a promise: If you ever get back to reality, you'll brush up on your vocabulary!

Keep falling until you reach PAGE 64.

You manage to open the door marked PRIVATE. It's pitch-black inside. You quickly shut the door to keep out the water.

A strong smell of stale popcorn fills the air. You feel around to find a light switch. You flip it on.

You're surrounded by bags of popcorn.

"Great!" you exclaim. "I didn't have time to get a snack." You tear open a bag and shove a handful into your mouth.

"Yuck!" You spit out the popcorn. "It's all soggy."

You glance down. Sure enough, water is seeping into the tiny room. The bags of popcorn are soaked.

"We still have to get to the projection room," Laura reminds you. She turns to open the door.

"It's locked!" she cries.

There's no way out. You had a chance to save the world and you blew it.

And what's worse, you're surrounded by bags of popcorn — and you can't even eat it!

THE END

"There's no time!" you repeat. You and Laura run toward the door.

And keep running.

And running.

Why can't we get to the door? you wonder. Why are we just running in place?

The painting laughs behind you. "No time, did you say? I have ways to take care of little problems like that." He laughs harder.

Now you get it. The painting has made time slow down. Way down. Stop. In fact, you could say your time just ran out.

You thought you had no time? Wanna bet? You have all the time in the world now. And you'll pay a heavy price all right — with your life.

For eternity!

THE END

"Maybe Blastovision is so awesome that people kept falling out of their seats," you suggest.

"Or maybe the movie is so lame that seatbelts are the only way to keep people in the theater," Laura teases.

You put a finger to your lips and shush her. You hope the movie isn't boring. Or you'll never hear the end of it.

You watch as the screen fills with a lush tropical forest. You sniff the air. It seems as if the room is filled with the smell of exotic flowers. Blastovision must have some kind of scent-maker.

The sound system is amazing. You hear birds calling, leaves and branches snapping — coming from all around you.

Off in the distance, you notice a black gorilla lumbering toward you. As he gets closer, you realize he is enormous. Gigantic. Huge. Big as a building! He towers over many of the jungle trees.

"That dude's big," Laura mutters.

BOOM! BOOM! BOOM! Your seat bounces with each plant-crushing step the monster ape takes.

Now you understand why this theater has seatbelts!

Hang onto your seat and turn to PAGE 17.

Laura drags you into the projection room. You slam the door and lock it.

"Whew!" You exhale. "That was close."

The humanigators pound on the door. "Hurry!" you cry. "Any minute now they'll break that door down."

You and Laura dash to the control panel. Every time the humanigators pound on the door, your heart pounds harder in fear. Your finger shakes as you reach out and hit the STOP button on the projector.

Will it work?

Turn to PAGE 69.

Agent Z double-checks your gear. Then, with a nod, he flips into the water. You and Laura follow him over the side.

Your eyes widen as you gaze at Dr. Aqua's underwater fortress. It looks exactly like a sunken castle. Tall turrets stand at the corners of the huge stone building. Grotesque gargoyles adorn the walls above the doorway.

As you swim closer you realize the windows are really portholes. And the fortress itself is actually an enormous submarine!

How are we ever going to get inside that? you wonder. And how will we ever get out?

Turn to PAGE 58.

You let out a sigh of relief. The person approaching is just an old, frail man. He wears a long overcoat and a funny tie.

"Need some help, youngsters?" he calls.

"Yes," you reply. "We dropped something on the other side of this panel. Do you know how to open it?"

"No one would know better than I," the old man declares. "I built this house."

"Do you know how we can get back to the movie theater?" Laura asks hopefully.

The man snorts. "Movies. Those newfangled inventions. Just a fad. Won't last. And noisy! Interrupts my rest. Having that movie theater next door keeps me up."

You and Laura grin at each other. Great! You'll be on your way home any minute.

With one sharp tap, the old man opens the panel. There they are — your glasses. You and Laura grab them.

"Now follow me," the old man instructs you.

Follow the man to PAGE 132.

How can you enter Agent Z's movie world? you wonder. But you have to find out. "We're with you!" you declare.

"Come on!" Agent Z reaches out his hand to you.

Right through the screen!

Awesome. You can't believe this is happening!

You take a deep breath and grab Agent Z's hand. You squeeze your eyes shut tight. You feel yourself being pulled forward. For a moment something presses hard against you. Then in a sudden rush, you burst through it.

That must have been the movie screen, you realize.

You open your eyes. You're standing on an un-damaged part of the concrete dam. Agent Z stands beside you. Laura is still in the movie the-ater. Her eyes are open wide in shock. She looks a little blurry. Of course, you think. I'm seeing her through the screen.

Together, you and Agent Z drag Laura into the movie.

Now that you're all in the same reality, turn to PAGE 5.

"Laura's right," you tell the twins. "We better not press our luck."

The twins grumble a bit, but they agree you should get back to searching for Aunt Kitty.

You pull the door open a crack. The coast is clear. No haunted armor.

"This dungeon is too creepy," you say. "Let's find our way back upstairs."

"Agreed," Laura says. Wendy and John nod.

Easier said than done. You wander for what feels like hours without ever finding a staircase. You have to keep on the lookout for the empty suit of armor. Luckily it clanks so loudly that you hear it coming long before it finds you.

You duck around a corner to keep out of sight. "There has to be a way up," you complain. You keep your voice low so the armor doesn't hear you.

"Not in this crazy house," Laura grumbles.

You sigh and lean against the wall.

"Look out!" John shouts.

Now what? Find out on PAGE 129.

That bouncing ball gives you the creeps. You dash down the stairs.

Only the stairs aren't there anymore!

Your feet fly out from under you as you reach for the wooden railing. It crumbles into dust in your hands. You slide down a slick, flat surface into complete darkness.

CRASH! You land on a pile of metal. "Oooomph," you grunt as the twins slam on top of you.

"Ouch!" Laura bangs into the twins.

"I've had enough rides for one day," you mutter, picking yourself up off the floor. Again.

"*Now* where are we?" Laura wails.

You stare at the pile of metal on the floor. Armor. You gaze around. You've seen rooms like this before. In books and movies. "I think we're in some kind of dungeon," you reply.

The twins stare at you, their eyes wide. "Why would Aunt Kitty have a dungeon in her house?" John asks.

"Good question —" you begin. A loud screeching noise interrupts you. Like the sound of fingernails on a blackboard.

And whatever is making the sound is coming closer.

Cover your ears and go to PAGE 15.

You and Laura sit in the grass and wait. The ape is captured. Now what? you wonder. Will you ever get back home?

The fat hunter approaches. "You youngsters were amazing. Such courage! Such fortitude!"

"Thanks," you murmur, blushing.

"And in return for your help, I will help you." He pulls two pairs of 3-D glasses from a pocket. "I believe these are yours. I found them as I was tracking the beast."

"Great!" you cry. "Now we can finally get home!"

You and Laura grab the glasses. You put them on.

The hunter was right. You're back in the movie theater as though nothing had happened.

Well, almost nothing.

You're amazed to discover that the audience is cheering you enthusiastically. "You were wonderful!" a woman cries.

You're even more surprised when you and Laura are nominated for Oscars for your performances in *Going Ape*.

But here's what's truly shocking:

Laura is nominated for Best Actress.

And all you get is a nomination for Best Supporting Role!

THE END

"We're on a break right now," the guy tells you. "Join us. We're hoping to have some snacks."

"Great!" You and Laura follow the man to a picnic table on the other side of the clearing. He introduces you to the crowd — about ten in all. They all have their masks pushed up on top of their heads.

"Cool!" Laura whispers. "I don't know how — but somehow we must have fallen into the movie set! Isn't this great?"

You nod. Now that you're not scared anymore, you notice you're hungry. "Did you say something about snacks?" you ask.

The man who invited you grins. "Now that you're here, we can have them."

You stare at him. You wonder what he means.

Uh-oh. Those sharp fangs that just slipped down over his lips should be a major clue.

Gulp! Turn to PAGE 95.

"Turn on all the dryers!" You dash to a machine. You fumble around in your pockets for change. You drop the quarters into the slot and turn the machine on high.

You rush to the next machine. Laura hurries down the row of dryers on the other side.

The water keeps rising.

"I'm out of quarters!" Laura shouts. "Do you have any more?"

You feel around in your pockets. Oh, no! You're out of quarters too. "Try the change-making machine," you yell. "Hurry!"

"But I don't have any money left!" Laura hollers back. "I spent it all on the movie!"

The water is up to your knees now. The heat from the dryers makes the laundromat steamy. You wipe sweat from your face.

Think, you order yourself.

Then again — don't bother. Accept it. This was a bad idea.

And now there's nothing you can do to *change* it.

So, to coin a phrase, this is

THE END.

"No way," you declare. "It would be a big fat mess."

You put on your 3-D glasses. Laura puts on hers. As the sights in front of you begin to shimmer and blur, you feel a heavy weight land on your shoulder.

"I'm coming anyway!" the gorilla roars.

A moment later, the three of you stand in the movie theater. What's left of it.

"What happened?" Laura gasps, staring at the piled rubble.

"Oh, no!" you exclaim. You gaze around at the terrible mess. "It was the ape. He was too big to fit. He smashed it all apart."

"Uh, sorry." The ape hangs his huge head sadly.

Sirens announce the arrival of police cars, fire trucks, and all kinds of emergency vehicles.

"Who's responsible for this disaster?" an officer demands.

The ape raises his hand. "Me," he confesses.

Turn to PAGE 74.

"Uh, where are we?" Laura asks in a shaky voice. "What happened?"

"I don't know. Maybe we fell into a basement under the movie screen," you suggest. Sounds reasonable. Only you don't really believe your own explanation.

A rustling sound makes your spine tingle. Wherever you are — you aren't alone!

"Who's there?" you call.

Before you can hear an answer, Laura grabs your arm. She shrieks in terror.

Rush to PAGE 68.

"Let's take our chances with the ape," you decide. "Maybe he just wants to get a better look at us."

Laura cowers beside you. One glance tells you she thinks you're crazy.

The ape brings his hand closer to his enormous face. Closer.

Closer to the drooling mouth. Closer to the gigantic teeth.

Boy, does this ape have bad breath.

Maybe you should rethink this plan.

You're startled by the sound of gunshots. The ape whirls toward the sound. His sudden movement causes you and Laura to tumble around in his palm.

"Yaaaaahhhh!" you scream.

Turn to PAGE 89.

You and Laura head for the river.

It's a mistake, you soon realize. "The plants are even thicker along the water," you complain.

She shrugs. "So it was a bad idea. What do we do now?"

You scan the area. "The river isn't moving too fast. I think it will be easier to travel *in* the water than next to it."

Laura agrees. The water is warm and only comes up to your knees. For a while you make progress.

A splashing sound catches your attention. "What's that?" you murmur. There's something gliding toward you in the water.

"Alligator!" Laura gasps.

Turn to PAGE 29.

A humanigator charges up. "What happened?" he demands.

You point at the damaged console.

He rushes over. "You did this?" he snarls.

You don't even bother to deny it. You nod glumly.

The humanigator's face twists into a huge smile. "Hooray!" he cheers.

Huh?

"What's going on?" Laura asks.

"You have rescued us from that evil Dr. Aqua," the humanigator explains. "We couldn't figure out a way to press any of the buttons." He holds up his webbed hand. "No fingers."

You figure these mutants aren't all that bright.

That's true. But they're bright enough to realize they need you and Laura to help them. So even though you're their hero, the humanigators keep you prisoner. They need you to navigate. They decide to have you take them on a long sight-seeing cruise. Which sounds good to you — until you realize that the sights they want to visit are swamps! And that you'll never get out of this movie.

Hey, it could be worse. So lighten up. And quit being such a stick-in-the-mud!

THE END

You clutch Laura's hands, holding them away from your throat. You stare into her eyes.

They look like the eyes of a zombie! She doesn't seem to recognize you.

"Kill," she murmurs. "I must kill."

You glance at the twins. They seem to be mesmerized by the spinning top. Or hypnotized, you realize. That must be what happened to Laura. The top hypnotized her into wanting to kill you!

You have to get the top to stop spinning! But how? If you release Laura's hands, she'll choke you. And now the twins are stretching their arms toward you, reaching to strangle you!

You notice the top has spun near your foot. Maybe you can kick it over. You also see another top, a red one. Maybe that will undo the evil work of the blue top. But to spin it, you'll have to let go of Laura's hands.

Which will it be?

If you kick the spinning blue top, turn to PAGE 124.

If you spin the red top, turn to PAGE 104.

You hurry to the laundromat. "Do you think Dr. Aqua wants to do his laundry?" Laura demands. "This is crazy."

"What do you find at a laundromat?" you challenge.

Laura rolls her eyes. "Lint? Lost socks?"

You glare at her. "Okay," she continues. "Soap. And . . . oh, right. Water."

"Bingo." You throw open the doors. A stream of water pours out, soaking your sneakers even more. You dart inside.

Water gushes from all the machines. "The place is flooding!" you exclaim.

A loud bang at the front door makes you jump. Dr. Aqua grins at you from the street. He padlocks the laundromat door.

"Oh, no!" Laura gasps. "We're trapped."

"And if we don't find a way to stop this flooding, we'll drown!" You scan the room. "I know! Let's turn all the dryers on full blast. That should dry up some of the water."

"Not enough," Laura argues. "We should try to find the main water supply and shut it off."

"Good idea," you agree. "But do we have time?"

Which should you do?

To hunt for the main water supply, turn to PAGE 26.

To turn on the dryers, turn to PAGE 49.

You hate breaking a promise. "Okay," you grumble. "Where's the paint?"

You find a paintbrush and a can of paint on the floor underneath the portrait. With a few strokes you fill in the man's eyes. "There. Done. Are you satisfied now?"

"Oh, thank you, thank you, thank you," the painting gushes. "I am overcome with emotion. I think I'm going to cry."

"Don't do that," you caution. "You'll ruin your eyes!"

"Well, what do we do now?" Laura demands. "We can't catch up to them. We don't even know for sure which way they went."

"I can help you there," the painting tells you. "Now that I can really see, I have super-vision. And the twins have locked Aunt Kitty up in a room just three doors away."

"Thanks!" You grab Laura's hand and dash down the hall.

"Just remember," the painting calls. "Sometimes it helps to shed a little light on a subject."

"Whatever," you mumble. You can't think about what the painting might mean right now. You have to save poor old Aunt Kitty. And somehow get out of this crazy movie!

The room three doors down is on PAGE 123. Get over there!

A voice crackles in your ear. "This is Agent Z. We have radios built into these wet suits. Can you hear me?"

"Sure can," you reply.

"Me too," you hear Laura say.

"We have two choices to gain entry," Agent Z continues. "There is a small vent near the main door. I'm too large to fit through. But one of you can climb in and then open the door for us to enter."

You gulp. You're a little smaller than Laura. If that's the plan — then you're it!

"Uh, what's the other idea?" you ask.

"I create a diversion. To chase me, they have to open up. Then you two sneak inside and destroy the flooding machine. But you'll have to do it without me."

Your heart pounds with fear. No matter which choice you make, you have to enter the fortress without Agent Z.

"We need to decide quickly," Agent Z tells you. "We don't want to give them a chance to detect our presence."

"I'll do whatever you decide," Laura's voice says.

To volunteer to climb in through the vent, turn to PAGE 111.

To have Agent Z create a diversion, turn to PAGE 114.

You stare at the twins.

"You're not going to take the word of some weird painting, are you?" John demands.

You glance over at Laura. Her face is white with fear. She points to the wall behind the twins.

Your eyes follow her finger. A large, ornate mirror hangs on the wall. Your mouth drops open as you understand.

The twins are standing right in front of the glass. But their reflection isn't in the mirror!

"They *are* vampires!" you cry. "And they're after Aunt Kitty. They tricked us into helping them find her."

"We'll just have to find her first," Laura declares.

"Good luck," John taunts. "Without this." He waves a large key at you. Then he and Wendy bolt from the room.

"They have the key to Aunt Kitty's hiding place! Hurry!" you exclaim. You and Laura sprint after the vampire twins.

"Hey," the eyeless painting shouts. "You promised you would paint my eyes."

"We don't have time," you argue.

"If you go back on your word," the man in the painting threatens, "you will pay a heavy price."

If you stop to paint the man's eyes, turn to PAGE 57.

If you think there's no time, turn to PAGE 39.

"Let's bag this movie," you shout over the deafening soundtrack. "This Blastovision is for the birds."

"You mean for the apes," Laura yells back.

"Yeah, let's not monkey around with it anymore!"

Laura groans at your bad joke as you scramble out of your seats. You stumble as the Blastovision makes the floor vibrate and roll. Your 3-D glasses fall out of your pocket. But you don't stop to pick them up. A row of seats crashes in front of you, blocking your way to the doors leading to the lobby.

"Over there!" You point out a set of side doors. As you hurry out, it sounds as if the movie theater is crumbling down around you.

You and Laura find yourselves back outside the theater. Lucky you! You get to start all over again.

Time to pick another movie!

To see Agent Z vs. Dr. Aqua, *turn to PAGE 9.*
To check out House of a Hundred Horrors, *turn to PAGE 120.*

You turn to face John. He sounds so serious. "What's up? Oh, of course!" You smack your hand against your forehead. "Aunt Kitty. We still have to find her."

"Forget Aunt Kitty," John tells you. He grins.

You stare at him — at his smile. His very toothy smile. You watch in horror as his teeth slip down over his lip. Two very sharp, gleaming, fang-like teeth.

"Vampires," you gasp. "You really are vampires!"

"Like you didn't see this coming a mile away," Wendy taunts. Her sharp fangs glisten. "And you think you're such a horror movie expert."

"What are you going to do now?" Laura's voice trembles. "Are you going to bite us?"

John shrugs. "Nah. We're after a lot more than you two."

Wendy nods. "There's no one here left to bite. But thanks to you — we have a whole new world of victims. Full of blood. The people in your world!"

John and Wendy put on the 3-D glasses. Your eyes widen as the twin vampires fade away to nothing and vanish.

You should have listened to the eyeless portrait. Instead you made a *grave* mistake!

THE END

62

You climb up the long, dark stairway to the tower. The circular tower room is made of stone. A tiny candle sits on the floor. Its flickering flame casts creepy shadows all around you.

You shiver. The tower room is damp and cold.

"Aunt Kitty," John calls. "We're here! We found you."

"EEEEEEKKK!" Laura shrieks, flinging her arms over her head.

"What's wrong?" you cry.

"Bats," she whispers.

You glance up. She's right! A large bat flutters overhead.

You shudder. You want to get out of here as quickly as you can. "Uh, Aunt Kitty, come out, come out wherever you — argh!"

Something pierces your neck. You grimace in agony. Two sharp needle points. Fangs! You crumple to the floor.

"Help!" Laura shrieks. "Something is biting me." She collapses. You see a bat hovering over her.

The bats! you realize. They must be *vampire* bats!

Go to PAGE 25.

"What?" you ask the giant gorilla.

"Take me with you," he begs.

"Wh-what do you mean?" you stammer.

The ape drops down to his knees. "Please. There's no future here for me. And it's so lonely here. I want to go someplace where I can have someone to talk to."

You shake your head. "But people would be as afraid of you in our world as they are here. I mean, giant talking apes aren't exactly normal."

"I don't care! I want to go! I want to! I want to!"

Wow! you think. This ape is going ape!

"Maybe we should let him come," Laura suggests. "It might be fun."

"Fun?" you repeat. "How do you want to explain going to the movies and coming home with one of the stars? And how are we going to feed him? Where will he stay?"

"Worry about that later," the gorilla urges. He bats his big brown eyes at you. "You won't regret it."

If you take the ape with you, turn to PAGE 113.

If you insist he stays in his own reality, turn to PAGE 50.

You hit the floor with a crash. Laura and the twins pile on top of you.

"Ouch! We're lying on something hard," you complain. You struggle to your feet and discover the mound you landed on is armor.

You gaze around the dark room. It seems to be some kind of dungeon. Before you can comment, you hear a screeching, groaning sound.

"What's that?" Laura asks, her voice trembling.

"I don't know," you reply. You fight back the fear rising in your chest. You swallow hard. "But I guess we better find out."

Check out the noise on PAGE 15.

The itching is getting worse. And the swelling is so bad you can barely breathe. All you can do is point at the hunter.

"Hey! Mr. Hunter," Laura calls. "Over here!" You and Laura crawl out of your hiding place.

The hunter whirls around. He smiles when he sees you.

"Looks like you have a bad case of creeping poison tree gunk," the hunter says. "I have the cure. Fix you right up."

The hunter reaches into one of his many pockets and pulls out a large, thick leaf. He takes a bite from the stem. Yellowish slime oozes out.

Your swollen nose crinkles in disgust. "That stuff stinks," you complain.

The hunter ignores you. He slaps the leaf on your arm. "Rub it all over, kid," he instructs you. "Or it's all over for you."

You do as he says. To your amazement, the stinky stuff makes you feel better instantly.

Thank the nice hunter on PAGE 112.

"Let's turn off the movie," you decide. "At least maybe we'll stop some of the flooding."

"Right," Laura agrees.

You swim out of the theater into the lobby. The flood is rising faster and faster. Soon it will completely fill the multiplex. You won't be able to keep your head above water.

Which means you won't be able to breathe! You have to shut off the film — and fast!

You scan the lobby. You wonder where the projection room is. You notice a spiral staircase leading up. "Do you think that leads to the projection room?" you ask Laura.

"Maybe it's in there," she replies, nodding toward a door marked PRIVATE. You can only see the top third of the door because of the flood.

Your muscles ache from treading water. Decide before it's too late!

If you go up the spiral staircase, turn to PAGE 130.

If you go through the door marked PRIVATE, turn to PAGE 38.

Your heart thumps in your chest. "D-d-did you say something?" you stammer.

"Of course I did," the painting announces. "We all speak. Except for those unfortunates without mouths."

This can't be happening, you think. Falling into movies. Talking paintings. What next?

"Beware of the vampires," the painting repeats.

Great. Something else to worry about.

"What vampires?" Laura demands.

"I will only tell you if you promise to paint in my eyes," the painting declares.

"We promise," you tell the painting. At this point, you'll say anything. You have to find out what the painting knows.

"Then I shall reveal the identity of the vampires." You stare, amazed, as he points at the twins. "There they are!" he cries. "And you must find Aunt Kitty before they do!"

The twins? Vampires? Your head swims. This is all too much.

"Don't believe him," another painting calls. "He's just trying to trick you into painting his eyes. How could he know who the vampires are?" the painting continues. "He can't even see."

If you think the twins are the vampires, turn to PAGE 59.

If you don't believe the eyeless painting, turn to PAGE 118.

"Look!" Laura screams. "It's them! How can that be?"

"Owww!" you cry. Laura is so freaked out she digs her nails into your arm. You have to pry her fingers off before you can turn to see where she is pointing.

Your mouth drops open in shock. Now you understand why Laura is cowering beside you.

Standing in front of you are the twins, John and Wendy. Only they aren't images from a movie screen. They're real. As real as you and Laura. And they *look* just as scared as you *feel*.

It's hard to believe — but there's only one explanation for what you're experiencing.

Somehow you fell right into the movie!

Turn to PAGE 119.

The movie clicks and shuts off. You gaze through the tiny window into the movie theater.

"It worked!" you exclaim. "The screen stopped gushing water!"

You yank the movie reel off the projector. You'll turn it over to Agent Z for safekeeping.

CRASH!

The door to the projection room crashes to the floor. A humanigator looms in the doorway.

You and Laura shrink backwards. There's no way out of the tiny room. Not with that mutant standing there.

He lunges for you. He grabs the movie reel from under your arm.

"Hey!" you cry. "Give that back!"

Turn to PAGE 93.

You really don't want to wander around in a jungle by yourself. "Okay," you declare. "We'll help you catch the monkey."

The hunter beams. "The giant man-eating monster gorilla, you mean."

"Whatever," you grumble.

You and Laura follow the hunter to the trap. It's a circular rope net spread over a deep pit.

"You want us to sit down there?" Laura demands. "The ape will squash us."

The hunter waves a hand at her. "Don't worry. The moment the ape steps onto the net, his weight triggers the springs." He points to several contraptions set around the clearing. "He's hoisted up into the air. He never really falls into the hole."

Laura still looks skeptical. You're about to call off the deal when the hunter nudges you with his rifle.

"Get into the trap," he orders. He shoves you and Laura roughly into the pit.

Turn to PAGE 101.

You and Laura stay low. You use the broad leaves and vines as camouflage. The path widens into a large clearing.

And in the center of the clearing is the giant ape!

"He's tied up," Laura whispers. "The hunters must have captured him."

The struggling gorilla throws his head back and howls. You stare at the huge creature. Your eyes widen. "Those aren't ropes," you gasp. "That's a giant snake!"

You're right. Wrapped around the ape is the biggest, thickest snake you've ever seen. The ape howls again. It's clear he's in pain. With every squeeze, the deadly snake comes closer to crushing him.

"Poor thing. We should help him," Laura murmurs.

You stare at her. "Are you nuts? Let's get out of here before either of those monsters notices us."

Laura shakes her head. "If we help the ape, maybe he'll help us. After all, he's the reason we're in this movie in the first place."

Hmmm. Maybe she has a point. What should you do?

To help the ape, turn to PAGE 77.
To run for your lives, turn to PAGE 126.

Laura drops down beside you. "Made it!" she exclaims.

You and Laura crouch by the roots of a large tree. You hope it will protect you from the ape's giant feet.

After a few minutes the creature lumbers away.

"So what do you think happened?" Laura whispers. "How did we end up in the movie?"

You shake your head. "I don't know. Maybe the Blastovision went wrong somehow. Or maybe those 3-D glasses had something to do with it. Too bad they fell off when the ape grabbed us."

"What do we do now?" Laura asks. You can tell by her voice she's scared.

You frown. "The way I figure it, we should get help from those hunters who were shooting at the ape. Or we should try to find the 3-D glasses. They must be around here somewhere."

So which will you do?

To search for the hunters, turn to PAGE 75.
To hunt for the 3-D glasses, turn to PAGE 85.

"We better go after Dr. Aqua," you decide. "He's out to flood the world. I bet he can do some serious damage."

You and Laura rush from the movie theater. "There he is!" You point at a Jet Ski zooming down the flooded street.

Dr. Aqua glances over his shoulder. "You'll never stop me!" he shouts. Then he vanishes around the corner.

The water in the street laps around your ankles. Your sneakers squish as you hurry onto Main Street.

"Where did he go?" You peer up and down the street. No sign of Dr. Aqua.

"He must have gone into one of the stores," Laura guesses. "It's the only way he could have disappeared so quickly."

She's right. But you notice the only places open are the electronics store and the laundromat.

"That narrows it down," you tell Laura.

"But which one should we check out?" she asks.

To check out the laundromat, turn to PAGE 56.
To investigate the electronics store, turn to PAGE 106.

"Did you say *me*?" the officer gasps. "You mean, you *talk*?"

News of the talking ape travels fast. Soon you're surrounded by photographers, journalists, and television producers. They all want to sign up the ape.

The ape loves the attention. He talks nonstop. Hour after hour of interviews.

Of course, he no longer talks to *you*. He will never forgive you for refusing to bring him into your reality.

Laura is his manager now. They're both billion-aires.

Yep. They're having more fun than a barrel of monkeys.

And it's making you bananas!

THE END

"I think we're going to need help getting back to the regular world," you decide. "Let's find those hunters."

You and Laura take off, heading toward where you heard the shots. It's tough going. You follow a narrow, twisting path. The thick vegetation makes it difficult to walk. Or to see more than a few inches ahead of you.

A terrible howling rises just beyond the bend up ahead.

"What's that?" Laura whispers. She clutches your arm.

"I don't know," you murmur. "But that's the only way forward. So I guess we're going to find out."

You and Laura creep toward the bend in the path. You try to move silently. If only you can keep your presence secret until you discover what is making that awful sound!

Peek around the bend on PAGE 71.

76

You don't think that the ape will be fooled into any dumb trap. You're out of there!

"Run for it, Laura!" you cry.

You race away as fast as you can. You figure the hunters will have their hands full dealing with the big ape. They'll forget all about you and Laura.

You slog through thick bushes and vines. It's really tough going.

Oh, well. At least no one is shooting at you, chasing you, or stomping on you.

Head for the river on PAGE 53.

You sigh. "Okay. We'll try to rescue the big ape. But how?"

Laura glances around. "I have an idea!" She grabs a handful of small brown pellets on the ground near a flowering shrub. She holds them up to show you. "This is a pepper plant. And you know what happens when you get pepper up your nose?"

"Duhhh. You sneeze. But what does this have to —" You smack a hand against your forehead. "Of course! If we make the ape sneeze, the sneeze will break the hold of the snake!"

Laura considers this. "Actually," she says, "I was thinking we would make the *snake* sneeze. But now I'm not so sure."

To make the ape sneeze, turn to PAGE 82.
To make the snake sneeze, turn to PAGE 97.

"What do you think you're doing?" the mutant demands.

"Wh-what do you mean?" you stammer.

"Why didn't you give the proper salute?" he says.

"Oh. Sorry." You try to imitate the clacking jaw and the sharp hand motion. Seeing your own scaly hand startles you. This is a very realistic costume, you think.

"Don't let it happen again," the mutant grumbles.

Relieved, you turn and start to walk away again.

"Hey! You!" Now it's the other humanigator.

You turn back around. "Yes?"

The humanigator circles you. You feel his hot breath on your neck. He rips something from your costume.

"Well, well, well. You're the first humanigator who sent himself out to get dry-cleaned!" He shoves a dry-cleaning ticket under your nose. "Can you explain this?"

"I'm very fussy about my appearance?" you say weakly.

Now the other humanigator closes in. Drool drips from his jaws. "Gee. I was just hoping for a snack."

Oh, well. We won't tell you about the eating habits of humanigators. It's too gruesome. And to describe it when it's about to happen to you just wouldn't be human!

THE END

John must have hit a secret panel. You grin. No haunted house is complete without one!

Your 3-D glasses make it seem as if you are falling with him. Laura must have the same feeling. She's leaning forward in her seat, just like you. Falling . . . falling . . .

Then suddenly — it's not just a feeling anymore! You really *are* falling!

You tumble forward with such force that you hit the ground with a hard *THUD*! Laura lands beside you.

You sit up, totally embarrassed. Everyone in the audience must think you and Laura are complete geeks to get so into the movie.

But as you glance around you make a terrifying discovery.

You aren't in the theater!

No audience. No movie screen. No popcorn containers and soda cups littering the aisles. Nothing.

Just a damp, musty smell and darkness.

Turn to PAGE 51.

"You'll never stop me!" Dr. Aqua's horrible laugh blares at you from all over the store.

You watch in terror as Dr. Aqua's face fades from the TV screen in front of you. Water bursts out of it! A torrent pours from all the TV screens, flooding the store.

"How did he do that?" Laura gasps.

"Who cares? Let's get out of here!" you scream. You dash to the door.

It's locked!

You dart across the store. "Maybe out the back!" you cry.

You and Laura hurry through the store. The water makes the floor slippery. You stumble and slide. You try to grab something to stop yourself from falling.

You grab one of the television sets. It crashes to the wet floor with you.

Oops. Big mistake.

Didn't anyone ever teach you that you shouldn't mix water and electricity?

PFFFT! ZAP! The TV set shorts out. The water conducts the electrical current. You and Laura fry.

What a shocking

END!

"Help us get back home," you reply.

You explain all about the movie theater and the 3-D glasses.

"Of course I'll help you get home." Aunt Kitty leads you back through the house. In no time at all she has found your 3-D glasses. You and Laura are on your way. Already you can see the movie world dissolving in front of you.

"If you're ever in the neighborhood, drop by," Aunt Kitty calls. "Oh, except when there's a full moon."

"D-d-did you say 'full moon'?" you stammer.

She chuckles. "I always have plans then," she explains. "It's funny. The full moon doesn't seem to have any effect on vampires. But they can't take the sun. Werewolves, on the other hand . . ."

As she fades away you hear her laughing. Or was that howling?

Well, you hope you never find out. Because you sincerely hope that this is truly

THE END.

"Do snakes even *have* noses?" you ask Laura. "I think we're better off with the ape."

You and Laura dash from your hiding place and hurl the peppercorns at the ape.

The big ape sniffles. He snuffles. Throwing his head back, he lets out a gigantic *aaaaaAAAAA-CHOOOOOOOOO!*

His whole body blows up like a balloon. The force of his sneeze knocks you and Laura over. He sneezes again.

"*Aaaaachhhoooooo!*" This time, as the ape's chest expands, the tightly wrapped coils of the snake burst apart. Gross! It's as if the snake is exploding.

It falls to the ground in pieces.

The ape blinks a few times. Then he focuses on you and Laura. Your heart pounds in terror as he snatches you off the ground.

"Oh, no," you groan. "Here we go again!"

Turn to PAGE 87.

"Empty," you murmur.

"Yikes!" Laura squeals.

The armor freezes. The visor snaps down with a click.

"Smart move," you mutter. "It heard you. Now it knows where we are!"

You're exactly right. The suit of armor slowly turns around. It heads straight for you.

"B-b-but it's just an empty suit of armor," Laura stammers. "It can't hurt us."

"Yeah, right," you mumble sarcastically. "Just like it can't walk. We better move it. If we don't get out of here fast, that armor is going to have four bodies to choose from. Ours!"

You dart across the room to a thick wooden door. With all four of you tugging you manage to get it open. Once inside, you shove the door shut.

Now all you can do is hope the armor gives up on you. . . .

Wait on PAGE 16.

"Two for *Going Ape!*" You hand the woman your money. You and Laura head for the theater. "The movie plot sounds kind of lame," you admit. "But I can't wait to check out Blastovision."

Laura nods. "I heard it's more awesome than 3-D."

You reach for the doors. You jump when bony fingers clutch your shoulder.

"What?" you yelp.

"Shush!" the usher who grabbed you orders. "Tickets, please."

You hand over the tickets. You feel dumb for being so jumpy. Imagine being scared by this sleepy-looking guy.

The usher yawns and gives you your ticket stubs. Then he holds out two pairs of 3-D glasses.

"What are those for?" Laura asks.

"You'll see," he replies. "But only use them when you really need them."

Find your seats on PAGE 7.

"We're going to need those 3-D glasses," you tell Laura. "They may be our only way home."

You know the glasses fell off when the giant ape grabbed you. You and Laura peer at the ground. You crawl around the bushes, searching.

BOOM! BOOM! BOOM! BOOM!

"Uh-oh," Laura mutters. "The ape is coming back."

"Keep looking for the glasses," you order. "We'll find them in plenty of time to get away."

Wanna bet?

You find them, all right. But before you can put them on, the giant ape's foot finds *you*!

Being squashed flat kind of throws a wrench in your plans to get home.

A *monkey* wrench.

THE END

You gaze around. The curved walls of the fortress are covered with gadgets. A console shows views outside different portholes. Another displays different locations inside the fortress.

"This must be part of the security system," Laura says.

"Yeah," you agree, gazing at the screens. "And it looks as if there are cameras everywhere."

As if on cue, you hear a clicking sound above you. You glance up. A camera is trained on you and Laura.

"Maybe we should destroy the console. It might buy us a little time," you suggest.

"Or maybe we should just run," Laura argues.

To destroy the console, turn to PAGE 6.
To just run, turn to PAGE 14.

The ape brings you up to his huge face. Right up to his enormous mouth.

"Is he going to eat us?" Laura wails.

Then, to your total shock — the ape kisses you!

"Yecchhh!" You wipe ape slobber off your face.

"Oh, thank you so much, dear friends," the ape gushes. "I owe you my life."

You're so stunned you fall down. Luckily the ape's palm is nice and soft.

"Y-y-you t-t-talk?" Laura stammers.

"Of course I do," the ape exclaims. "You thought I could only grunt? I must be a pretty good actor!" Then he sighs sadly. "But I'm tired of always playing the bad guy. I'm always typecast because of how I look."

You feel bad for the big gorilla. You're glad you rescued him.

"Now, is there anything I can do for you?" the ape asks.

"Well, actually," you begin, "there *is*. . . ."

Turn to PAGE 34.

"We'll stick with you," you tell the hunter. At least we'll have some help with the ape, you figure.

"Jolly good!" The hunter beams. "Stay close. I spotted him just a few miles down."

As you and Laura follow the hunter through the jungle, he explains his plan. "Once we find the ape, I'll signal the rest of the hunting party to get the nets into place. Then you two drive him to the trap!"

This plan sounds a little better than being bait. But not much.

Turn to PAGE 19.

You grab onto Laura to try to stay steady. "Where are those gunshots coming from?" you demand.

"In the preview, there was a hunter in the movie," Laura explains. "It must be him."

"I think we might be able to make it down safely while the ape is distracted," you whisper. "Let's climb down a tree."

"Those branches don't look very sturdy," Laura points out. "I think we're better off grabbing one of those thick vines and swinging to safety."

More gunshots ring out. You need to decide fast! The ape is worrying about the hunters right now. But any minute he'll remember about you . . .

Do you climb down a tree? Turn to PAGE 30. Or swing on a vine on PAGE 90.

Laura is right. Swinging on a vine will be a lot faster than climbing down.

You grab a thick, sturdy-looking vine. Laura does the same. You clutch it tightly and wrap it around your legs.

You nod at Laura. Then you both leap from the ape's palm.

"Aaaaaaaaaaaeeeeeeeeoooooooeeeeeahhhhhhh!" You can't help it. You let out a Tarzan yell.

You swing through the air. The trees rush by you in a blur. You hope you don't smash into anything!

The vine jerks to a stop abruptly a few feet above the ground. You drop down onto the squishy earth.

Turn to PAGE 72.

You and Laura slip on the glasses.

Suddenly you're back in your seats at the movie theater!

"We did it!" Laura exclaims. "We're back home!"

You stare at the screen. At Aunt Kitty and the twins. They smile and wave at you.

"See you soon!" Aunt Kitty calls.

"Real soon," the twins add. They grin.

Not if I can help it, you think. It was really bizarre to be trapped in that haunted-house movie.

"Let's go!" you tell Laura. You scramble out of your seats and down the aisle. You and Laura hurry out of the theater.

Outside, you blink in the bright sunlight. You catch a quick glimpse of a poster at the entrance.

"Oh, no," you gasp.

"What's wrong?" Laura asks.

But you can't answer. All you can do is point a trembling finger at the poster. It reads:

COMING SOON: *RETURN TO THE HOUSE OF A HUNDRED HORRORS*.

THE END

Huge, drooping eyes glare down at you. A wild thatch of black-and-red hair stands straight up on the man's head. His mouth is a twisted grimace.

You back away in terror. You feel Laura shaking beside you.

The man takes a step toward you. He grabs his chin — and shoves his face on top of his head!

You shut your eyes tight. "Aaaaaaahhhh!" you and Laura shriek together.

"What gives?" the man asks.

You open your eyes.

Hey! That's not his face — it's a mask!

"You kids are really jittery," the man comments. He gives you an easy smile. "Anyone would think you believed we really were cannibals. Didn't anyone tell you we're making a movie?"

"S-s-s-sure," you stutter. "We knew that. Of course!"

Yeah, right. Turn to PAGE 48.

You leap at the humanigator. But the slippery floor makes you fall. Water is beginning to seep up to this level.

It gives you an idea.

"We have to ruin the film!" you shout to Laura.

She hurls herself at the humanigator. You grab onto its tail. Laura clings to its back, kicking at its arm. Finally the struggling humanigator drops the film reel.

It lands in the water.

The humanigator gasps.

"Just to be sure . . ." Laura yanks a small bottle of nail polish remover from her backpack. She dumps it onto the film.

"Nooooooo!" The humanigator howls in agony. You and Laura duck out of the way of its thrashing tail. You watch in amazement as the mutant completely fades away.

Turn to PAGE 125.

You quickly find a painting of a man wearing funny little glasses. You carefully lift it from the wall.

"There it is!" Laura shouts. She reaches into a small hole behind the painting and pulls out a shiny gold key.

"Way to go!" John cheers.

"Let's go rescue Aunt Kitty," Wendy cries.

You return the painting gently to its spot. You check to be sure it hangs straight. Then you face the others. "So how do we get to the tower?" you ask.

A deep voice replies. "I can tell you."

You whirl around. The painting! The painting spoke to you!

The man in the painting peers at you through his funny little glasses. "Pull the velvet rope over my head to get to the tower," he instructs you.

You glance up. Sure enough, there is a rope hanging from the ceiling above the painting. You give it a sharp tug.

And gasp!

The wall beside the painting slides open, revealing a long stairway.

To the tower!

What are you waiting for? Get to the tower on PAGE 62.

You grab Laura's hand. You start to back away very slowly. But the ten others circle around you.

You're surrounded.

By a group of guys with fangs.

"But you said you weren't cannibals!" Laura screams.

The man laughs. "We're not. We're vampires."

"That's impossible!" you argue. "It's light out. Vampires can't survive in the sun."

The group of vampires laughs. "We're *movie* vampires," one of them explains. "We're used to working under bright lights. Over the years we've learned to withstand even the sun."

"But this isn't even a vampire movie!" Laura yells.

The first vampire shrugs. "Do you know how hard it is to make a living these days? We're usually in *House of a Hundred Horrors*. But we decided to make some extra money by doing part-time work over here."

There's no escape, of course.

You've always enjoyed snacks at the movies. You just never thought you'd *be* one!

THE END

The screen is completely black. The thunderous sounds have stopped. You can't see the ape anymore.

"What a gyp!" you cry. "Where's the movie?" You wipe some sweat from your forehead. The air is hot and heavy with moisture. "What happened to the air-conditioning?" you complain. "It feels like a sauna in here."

"Or a jungle," Laura offers.

"Do you smell something gross?" you ask.

But before Laura can answer, you're snatched from your seats!

Turn to PAGE 137.

"Let's go for the snake," you say. Armed with peppercorns, you and Laura creep up to the battling pair of giant creatures. You don't want them to notice you. Otherwise they might decide to fight you instead!

Just one problem. "Which end is which?" you whisper to Laura. "Where's the snake's nose?"

"I can't tell," Laura murmurs.

"Where do we throw the peppercorns?" you demand. You're starting to get nervous. You and Laura are now in plain sight.

"I don't know," she replies.

"That's it! Just throw!" You hurl the peppercorns toward the snake. You hope some of them land near its nose.

Too bad you forgot about the breeze.

"Aaaachooo!" You and Laura start sneezing uncontrollably as peppercorns fly into your face.

You instantly attract the snake's attention. It unravels itself from the ape and slithers toward you.

Well, why shouldn't it? You and Laura are much easier to deal with than a gigantic gorilla.

Besides, you're already well seasoned. Now all the snake needs is a little salt!

THE END

You stare at Agent Z. He must be crazy. How can two real kids like you and Laura enter his movie world?

"Uh, we'll do what we can here, sir," you tell Agent Z.

Laura nods. "You can count on us."

"Good! I'll go to his fortress and track down his next target." Agent Z zooms away.

The water is halfway to the ceiling. You and Laura struggle to stay afloat as the screen continues pouring water into the theater.

"Wow," you murmur. "The Agent Z movie is spilling over into our real lives. This is bizarre." And scary! But you don't say that out loud.

"What do you think we should do?" Laura asks. "Go after Dr. Aqua ourselves? Or turn off this stupid movie?"

Good question. So which is it?

Turn off the movie on PAGE 66.
Try to find Dr. Aqua on PAGE 73.

What do the notes spell?

If you think they spell DEADFACE, *turn to PAGE 133.*

If you think they spell FADED AGE, *turn to PAGE 32.*

"Okay," you tell Laura. "I'll go left. You go right."

BOOM BOOM! BOOM BOOM! The gorilla is almost upon you.

"Ready? Set? GO!"

You and Laura take off at top speed. The ape lurches forward, trying to grab you. You make a hard left, swerving around his gigantic foot. You notice he does a double take as Laura sprints around his right.

The gorilla twists and turns, trying to grab you both at the same time. His head whips back and forth trying to watch you both at once.

He's like a giant semitruck trying to make a sharp turn, you realize. He's just too big to move fast.

Uh-oh. He's also about to jackknife!

"ROOOOAAARRRRR!"

The gorilla whirls his huge arms, trying to maintain his balance. He can't. With a deafening *THUD* he crashes to the ground.

Did we say *THUD*?

We meant *SPLAT*. Because unfortunately, a toppled giant ape covers a lot of ground.

And now, so do you. . . .

THE END

You and Laura huddle in the dark dirt hole. "Once the ape is captured, I'm sure the hunter will help us find our way home," you assure Laura.

You hope.

Several long minutes pass. No ape.

"What if the ape doesn't show up?" you call to the hunter. "How long do we have to stay down here?"

"Does the ape even know we're in here?" Laura hollers.

The hunter pokes his head over the hole. "Terribly sorry. You're absolutely right." He vanishes for a moment.

You turn to Laura hopefully. "Maybe he'll let us out now."

"I forgot the ape-attractor!" the hunter exclaims, reappearing above you.

"The what?" you demand.

Stinky green oil pours down on you and Laura.

"Ick!" she squeals. "What a smell!"

The hunter chuckles. "It's irresistible to most jungle animals. The ape should be here any second."

Turn to PAGE 3.

"Give up," Agent Z calls again.

"Never!" Dr. Aqua holds his arm in the air. He clutches something in his webbed hand.

"A grenade!" you whisper. "He's going to blow up the dam!" You grin. This should be exciting.

BLAM!

The flash from the explosion nearly blinds you. You throw your hands up to cover your eyes. "That sure seemed real," you murmur.

A rushing, pounding, roaring sound makes you drop your hands from your face. You gasp. Laura grabs your arm.

"The water!" she screams. "It's coming *out* of the movie screen!"

A torrent of water washes over the dam — and into the theater! You can't believe it!

The audience goes crazy. People dart frantically up the aisle. They bang into one another. They knock each other down. They shriek and scream, slipping in the rising water.

You climb onto the back of your seat. The water comes up to your neck. "How can the movie turn real like this?" you scream.

"Look out!" Laura shouts.

Turn to PAGE 134.

You gasp in terror. Coffins lie scattered around you. Cobwebs hang from the ceiling. And is that a — skeleton?

"Welcome to my home," the old man cackles. He shuffles over to the trapdoor and slams it shut. Then he pushes a large coffin over it.

"Now if only that movie theater weren't so noisy," he grumbles, "I'd be able to get plenty of rest."

You stare at him as he fades away to a mere outline, then vanishes into the coffin.

You and Laura shriek and run to the door. Huge chains hang padlocked across it.

It looks as if you're going to miss the end of the movie.

Well, actually, this *is* the end of the movie. And of you!

THE END

You release Laura's hands and grab the red top. With a quick flick, you give the top a twirl.

Laura freezes.

"Laura!" you cry. "Snap out of it!"

Laura's knees buckle and she collapses. The twins flop onto the floor behind you.

POP! BANG!

You whirl around at the noise. It sounds like firecrackers. Your mouth drops open.

The two tops have exploded, leaving nothing behind but tiny wisps of dust.

"Wh-wh-what happened?" Laura murmurs. Her eyes flutter open.

John groans and stretches. Wendy sits up, blinking her eyes. "What's going on?" she asks.

"Playtime is over," you declare. "Let's get out of here."

Hurry to the room marked MUSICAL INTERLUDE on PAGE 8.

You throw open Door Number 5.

"Aunt Kitty!" the twins cry, dashing into the room. "We've found you!"

You stare at the little old woman sitting by a window. You recognize her from somewhere. Then it hits you.

She was at the movie theater! She gave you the 3-D glasses!

"Thank you for helping us," John says.

"And now we'll help you," Wendy adds. "Aunt Kitty, these two want to get back home."

You gaze at Aunt Kitty. You hope she knows how to get you out of this movie and back to reality. *Your* reality!

You cross your fingers for luck.

Aunt Kitty reaches into a large handbag sitting at her feet. She pulls out two pairs of 3-D glasses. "I think you dropped these," she says. "They should do the trick."

Will they?

Turn to PAGE 91.

106

You approach the electronics store. The fire hydrant in front of it gushes water into the street. "That proves it," you whisper to Laura. "He must have come this way."

You tiptoe inside. "Keep low," you murmur, ducking below the counter. "We don't know where he is."

"I'm right here!" Dr. Aqua's voice booms. "And here! And here! And here!"

You cry out. Laura gasps.

Dr. Aqua's face stares out at you from every TV screen in the store!

Don't change the channel! Turn to PAGE 80.

This guy is nuts. You don't want to be bait for a giant ape!

"Run for it!" you yell. You give Laura a shove and the two of you dash into the bushes.

"You'll be sorry!" the hunter calls after you.

You hope he's wrong.

You and Laura battle your way through the thick vegetation. It's rough going. You wish you had worn long pants. Your legs are getting all scratched up by the prickly bushes.

The tiny path you follow comes to an abrupt end. You turn around and face Laura. "What do we do now?" you ask.

She shades her eyes with her hand and gazes around. "Do you hear water?" She points through the trees. "There's a river down there. Maybe we should see where it leads."

You peer in the direction of the water. You could keep heading through the jungle. You had a good view from the ape's palm. You noticed a few huts on the other side of the jungle.

But the plants seem less thick down by the river. It would make walking easier. Maybe that's the way to go.

To keep slogging through the jungle, turn to PAGE 135.

To go down to the river, turn to PAGE 53.

Wendy is right. You might find something useful in the Helter-Skelter Drawer. Or really cool. You pull the drawer open again and pull out —

"A toothbrush!" You stare at the object in your hand.

Laura snorts. "Oh, yeah, that will come in handy."

You toss the toothbrush aside and reach in again. Only this time you don't feel anything.

"There's got to be something else in there," you mutter. You reach further into the drawer. So far you practically crawl inside the dresser.

"Yeeeoooooowwch!" Something bit you!

You try to yank your arm back. But whatever has you in its teeth grips you tightly. You feel yourself being dragged into the dresser.

Laura and the twins try to pull you out. But it's no use. The fanged creature is too powerful. With a sharp tug, you are yanked all the way into the dresser. The drawer shuts with a *SLAM*!

Oh, well. Maybe the next person to reach into the Helter-Skelter Drawer will have enough luck for both of you.

Maybe the next person will pull out — YOU!

THE END

You and Laura scurry into seats in the front row. Spooky music fills the theater as the movie begins.

Awesome! The glasses *do* make the haunted mansion look real. You feel as if you could touch the gnarled, twisted bushes and step up onto the creaky old porch.

The movie is about a pair of twins, Wendy and John, who have come to visit their aunt Kitty. No one has seen her for many years.

No wonder, you think. Who would want to hang around in that ugly old place? But it's the perfect setting for a scary movie. You feel Laura shiver beside you.

John reaches for the front door. It swings open by itself. And the moment the twins step inside, the door slams shut behind them. They frantically rattle the doorknob.

Locked!

"Big surprise," you murmur. You know how these movies work.

"Aunt Kitty," Wendy calls. "Aunt Kitty, where are you?"

She and her brother try to pry open the door. No luck. Furious, John pounds the wall beside the door with his fist.

The wall shifts under his hand! He stumbles forward into blackness. "Help!" he cries. "Something is sucking me in!"

Go to PAGE 79.

You leap back. The whip cracks inches from your face.

"Hey!" you cry. You could almost feel the sting of the whip on your cheek. That was a little too close.

The hunter still doesn't respond. Instead he steps forward and bends over. He lifts a huge black spider off the ground. He dangles it in front of you. It's split in two.

You gulp.

"Have to watch out for these critters," the hunter informs you. "One bite and it's all over." He flings the deadly creature into the bushes.

The chubby man pokes you with the whip. "What are you doing here, anyway? Your clothing is very odd."

"The ape dragged us into this movie," you blurt out. "See, we put on these 3-D glasses and —"

The hunter shakes his head. "You must have heatstroke," he says sadly. "You're not making any sense!"

"We just want to get home. Can you help us?" Laura pleads.

The hunter studies you both. "Perhaps," he murmurs finally. "But only if you help me capture the gorilla first. Let me use you as bait."

You stare at the hunter. Is this guy serious?

Turn to PAGE 4.

"I'll climb in through the vent," you declare. At least this way, once you get the door open, Agent Z and Laura will be there to help defeat the humanigators.

"It's a dangerous mission," the superagent informs you. "But to help you, I've planted a humanigator disguise inside the vent."

You feel better hearing that.

Agent Z instructs you on how to get to the main door. He tells you the special code to open the door without setting off the alarm. Then he gives you a quick salute.

I never knew a person could sweat underwater, you think as you swim up to the vent.

Well, here goes.

You crawl into the vent.

And into evil Dr. Aqua's fortress.

Turn to PAGE 136.

112

"Thank you," you gush. You're thrilled to see your skin return to its normal color.

The hunter waves a hand at you. "Think nothing of it," he tells you. "But now there is something you can do for me."

You glance at Laura and sigh. "Be bait to catch the big ape," you mumble.

"No, no, no, dear child. That was a foolish idea. I have a new plan. We'll track the creature together. Then you'll lead him into a trap. I want to bring him back alive!"

Laura frowns. "Isn't that basically the same thing as being bait?"

"Listen, girlie," the hunter snaps. "Like it or lump it. That's the plan. Unless you'd rather go it alone." A sly smile crosses his face. "But I wouldn't recommend it. This jungle is *full* of cannibals."

Great. A giant ape — or cannibals.

You don't like either of those choices.

But they're the only ones you have!

To risk the cannibals, turn to PAGE 36.
To track the ape, turn to PAGE 88.

The ape looks so pathetic that you can't resist. "Come on," you tell him. "But be really careful."

The ape holds you and Laura in his palm. You put on the 3-D glasses. The world goes black.

The next thing you know, you're back in the movie theater! Cool! It worked!

Your parents totally freak when you bring the ape home. But he's so polite and helpful around the house, they give in.

At first, it's fun having a giant talking gorilla as a pal. But soon he develops a really annoying habit. He constantly, well, *apes* everything you do.

You beg him to stop copying you, but he just won't quit. It's driving you crazy.

But it's not really his fault, you know.

After all, monkey see, monkey do.

THE END

"You create a diversion. We'll sneak inside and find the flooding machines," you tell Agent Z.

"Definitely," Laura's voice agrees.

"Great. But work fast," Agent Z cautions. "The fortress is full of sensors. They'll detect your presence quickly."

You gulp. You try to keep your voice steady. "So, what now?"

"Now I get their attention." You can almost hear Agent Z smiling. "And you sneak in as they come to get me."

Agent Z gestures for you to position yourselves flat up against the wall beside the entrance. He aims a large underwater laser gun at the door and fires. Then he fires again!

Just as the door slides open, Agent Z punches a button on the belt of his wet suit. He zooms away so fast you can barely see him.

Dozens of humanigators swarm out of the fortress in pursuit. As the door begins to automatically close, you and Laura slip inside.

"Made it," you murmur. "Now for step two."

Turn to PAGE 86.

"Don't wimp out on me now," you holler over the deafening noise. "It's just a movie."

You sound a lot braver than you feel. But you're not going to let some special effects freak you into leaving!

"In fact," you declare, "this Blastovision is too tame. I'm going to put on my 3-D glasses to make it more realistic."

You pull the 3-D glasses from your pocket. Your hands shake. You can't tell if it's with fear or because the theater is rocking so violently.

You turn to Laura. "I dare you." You grin. You know she can't resist a dare.

She grits her teeth. Then she yanks her glasses out of her pocket. "Fine. I will if you will."

You both put on your glasses. You face the screen.

Your mouth drops open in shock.

Turn to PAGE 96.

116

"Uh, we're kind of in a hurry," you tell the twins. "I think we better just stick to finding the glasses."

"If they don't want to help us," Wendy comments, "why should we bother helping them?" She spins around and storms out.

John shakes his head. "I wouldn't wander around alone in this place if I were you." Then he hurries after his sister.

You gaze at Laura. "Now what?" you mutter.

Laura stares at the wall. "I think I can see the outline of the secret panel. Maybe we can get it open somehow."

You and Laura set to work trying to reopen the panel. You are interrupted by the sound of footsteps behind you.

Have the twins returned? Aunt Kitty?

Or —

Laura clutches your arm in fear.

Slowly, you turn around.

Turn around to PAGE 43.

You twirl the top. The twins stand behind you, watching it spin. Laura hovers nearby.

You stare at the top spinning around and around and around and around. All of your attention is on the tiny, whirling toy.

Around. Around. Around. Around.

You forget where you are. You don't hear or see anything but the blue top. You feel as if your mind is going blank.

Until you feel a pair of strong hands around your throat!

"Gack," you choke out. You pry the fingers from your neck. "Laura," you gasp, "help me!"

But as you gaze up at your attacker you realize Laura won't save you.

She's the one choking you!

Turn to PAGE 55.

118

You stare at the twins. It just doesn't make any sense, you decide. If they really were vampires, they would have bitten us already.

"Thanks for the warning," you tell the painting. "But we'll stick with the real people. Not portraits."

You smile at the twins. They seem relieved that you didn't believe the eyeless man in the painting.

"You're making a mistake!" the painting cries. "And what about your promise? My eyes! You have to paint my eyes."

"Wacko painting," you mutter as you head down the hall. You feel a little guilty about going back on your word, but, hey — it's not as if he's real or anything.

Finally you come to a room that seems familiar. "This is where we started from!" Laura cries.

She's right. You're back at the front door! "The 3-D glasses must be around here somewhere," you exclaim.

"Got it!" A pair of glasses dangle between John's fingers. Wendy gleefully waves the other pair in her hand.

"Great!" You and Laura hug each other. "Now we can get back to reality!"

"Not so fast," John announces.

Turn to PAGE 61.

"Who are you?" John demands. "And what have you done with Aunt Kitty?"

"And why did you lock us in the house?" his twin yells.

"Whoa! Slow down." You hold up your hands to stop their accusations. "We didn't do anything."

"Yeah," Laura adds. "We don't even know how we got here."

You quickly explain about the movie and the 3-D glasses. Finally the twins believe you.

"I have a feeling we'll need those glasses to get back home," you say. "But they fell off on the other side of that secret panel. Do you know how to open it?"

"No," John admits. "But I'm sure Aunt Kitty does. If you help us find her, we'll help you find your way back home."

Laura raises an eyebrow. You know that expression. That means she isn't sure what to do.

Maybe you should figure out how to get back on your own. After all, this movie is probably all about terrible things that happen while the twins search for their aunt.

But you don't know if you'll be able to open the panel without help.

What should you do?

If you agree to help find Aunt Kitty, turn to PAGE 2.

If you decide to find your way out alone, turn to PAGE 116.

You head for the theater showing *House of a Hundred Horrors*.

"Are you sure you want to see this?" Laura asks nervously. "It sounds kind of scary."

"The scarier the better." You give Laura a wicked grin. "Anyway," you add reassuringly, "it's just a movie. If you wimp out, just cover your eyes."

You reach for the door when a hand grabs your shoulder. "Where do you think you're going?" a voice behind you demands.

You whirl around. A little old lady stands in front of you.

"Where do you think you're going," the woman repeats, "without these?" She hands you and Laura each a pair of 3-D glasses. "They'll make the movie seem more real."

"Cool!" you exclaim. You've always wanted to see a 3-D movie. You and Laura put on the glasses. You turn to thank the woman.

She's gone!

Hey! The movie's starting. Hurry to your seats on PAGE 109.

"I'm going to catch that bouncing ball," you announce. "I have to see how it bounces itself."

You wait in the hallway until the ball is almost upon you. You stretch out your arms and leap up, just as the ball reaches the highest point in its bounce. "Gotcha!" you cry.

POPPPPPP!

"Yahhh!" The moment your hands touch the ball, it explodes!

You are amazed that you weren't hurt by flying bits of the ball. Glancing down at your hands, you discover a tiny piece of paper. It must have been inside the ball.

You read it to the others. "'Please help me! I've been locked in the North Tower by vampires. You will find the key behind a painting of a man with pince-nez. Signed, Aunt Kitty.'"

"We have to save her!" Wendy cries.

"Let's find the portrait with the pince-nez. Follow me!" You charge down the hallway.

Then it hits you. You turn and face the others. "What's pince-nez?" you ask sheepishly.

If you think pince-nez is a hat with a tassel, go to PAGE 37.

If you think it means funny little glasses, turn to PAGE 94.

122

You and Laura easily fit into the enormous ape's palm. Laura is too terrified to speak. She points down. Way down.

You gaze at the tops of jungle trees. You are definitely on an express ride up. Then Laura tugs your arm again. This time she's pointing up at the ape.

And now *you're* too terrified to speak. You stare into the drooling, gaping jaws of the ape.

"Let's jump!" Laura screams. "Before he eats us!"

"Are you crazy?" you shout. "Look how far up we are!"

"So we should just be gorilla snacks?" Laura demands.

"You'd rather be smashed to pieces on the ground down there?" you retort. "Besides, maybe he won't eat us."

What should you do? Those teeth are coming closer and the ground is getting farther away!

If you jump, turn to PAGE 127.
If you wait, turn to PAGE 52.

Your heart beats faster as you enter the room. It is dark inside, except for a thin ray of sunlight shining through the curtains of a tall window.

But even in the dim shadows you can see you are too late. The twins clutch a terrified woman between them. "You'll never save her now," John taunts.

"And you'll never find your way home, either." Wendy laughs meanly.

You've got to do something — fast. You glance around the dark room, trying to find a weapon. An idea. Anything!

Then you remember the strange words of the painting. Of course. *A little light on the subject!* Vampires can't survive being exposed to the sun!

You dart to the window.

Yank open the curtains on PAGE 128.

You kick out your foot as hard as you can, never letting go of Laura's hands. The spinning top clatters to the floor.

For a moment, Laura's grip relaxes.

"Phew!" you exhale. "Glad that's over."

Then you feel *four* hands grab you from behind. The twins!

"Hey!" you cry. Then you notice the top. It's spinning again. All on its own.

And you know what? Every time you knock it over or try to stop it, it starts up again. And again and again and again. Once the spell starts it cannot be broken.

And whose big idea was it to twirl the harmless little top? Oh, right — yours!

This (gasp! gag!) topsy-turvy ending has you all choked up.

THE END

"I think we did it," Laura gasps.

You get up off the floor. The water has disappeared. You peer through the tiny window.

The flood has vanished. It all evaporated when the film was destroyed.

You really did it!

You notice something strange when you leave the movie theater. The poster advertising *Agent Z vs. Dr. Aqua* has been replaced.

You approach the woman selling tickets at the booth. "Excuse me," you ask. "What happened to the new Agent Z movie?"

She frowns. "What new Agent Z movie?"

You turn to stare at Laura. "I guess when we destroyed the film we made everything disappear," you murmur.

Laura's face goes pale. "As if it never existed at all," she whispers. "Weird!"

Tough luck. You saved the world, but you ruined a perfectly good movie!

THE END

"Let's run for it," you urge.

You grab Laura's hand and dash back into the jungle. You don't worry about being quiet. You figure the ape and the snake are too busy to come after you.

WRONG!

Your rustling and crashing through the undergrowth attracts the snake's attention. It releases the ape and slithers after you.

Face it. Unlike you and Laura, the snake was built for speedy travel through the jungle. It reaches you and Laura very quickly.

First the snake trips you. Then it wraps itself around you and Laura. Then it . . .

Well, you don't need to know the rest. Let's just say that great big hug it gives you definitely isn't a sign of friendship.

But you *are* the snake's main squeeze!

THE END

"When I count to three," you instruct Laura, "we'll jump. One . . ."

"Three!" Laura leaps from the ape's hand. You follow her.

Didn't anyone ever tell you to look before you leap? Okay, so let's say you manage to survive the fall. As if . . .

But just pretend. There's still the little problem of the man-eating critters living in the jungle. They don't like intruders dropping out of the sky and into their nests. And make no mistake about it — they're *kid*-eating too.

So — you may have escaped being a gorilla snack, but you still end up on the low end of the food chain in

THE END.

Sunlight streams into the room as you pull the velvet curtains with all your might. You choke on the thick dust that flies from the heavy fabric. Laura tugs the other side.

"Yahhhhhhhhh!" The twins shriek in agony. You turn and watch the horrifying sight.

Smoke rises from John's and Wendy's bodies. Their hair curls up and blackens as if it's burning. They double over in pain, their skin melting off their bones.

The stink is nearly unbearable as the two vampires crackle and burn in front of you. You cover your ears to try to stop the sound of their agonizing screams. Finally nothing is left of them but two piles of ashes.

"You saved me! You saved this house!" Aunt Kitty rushes to you. She throws her frail arms around your neck.

"This was once a wonderful place to live. Until those two came." She nods toward the ashes. "They scared everyone away — those they didn't turn into vampires! I was so lonely. People even thought that I was a vampire. Me!"

You and Laura laugh too. You're glad you were able to save this sweet old lady.

"Now whatever can I do to repay you?" she asks.

Name your reward on PAGE 81.

John reaches for your arm and yanks you forward. "You almost fell into an iron maiden!" he cries, pointing behind you.

"A what?" Laura asks.

John explains that an iron maiden is an ancient torture device. You stare at the coffin-shaped box. It's lined with sharp metal spikes inside. Anyone shut up inside that thing would be pierced right through!

You shudder. "Let's get out of here," you urge, backing away from the iron maiden.

"But how?" Laura demands. "We've been searching and searching for a way out. Nothing."

A voice from above makes you jump. "If getting upstairs is what you'd like," it announces, "climb in the box but avoid the spikes."

"Who said that?" you demand.

Wendy points a shaking finger above the iron maiden.

"A parrot?" you exclaim. You stare up at the birdcage swinging from the ceiling. "What is a parrot doing down here?"

"What is *anything* doing down here?" Laura comments.

"More important," John adds, "why is it telling you to get into the iron maiden to go upstairs?"

Turn to PAGE 28.

You swim over to the spiral staircase. You grab onto the railing and hoist yourself up. By the top step, you can stop swimming. The water hasn't reached the second level. Yet.

You glance around. The deserted snack bar covers the back wall. More theaters. Hmmm . . .

"There!" Laura points to a door marked PROJECTION ROOM.

You dart across the upper lobby.

Uh-oh. You spot a terrifying reflection in the mirrors lining the walls.

Three humanigators are heading up the stairs.

You know from the previews that Dr. Aqua created these monstrous creatures. They walk upright like humans and have arms and legs. But they can also swim like alligators.

Their eyes are lidless. They have no hair — only scales. Long, powerful alligator tails thrash behind them. And instead of noses, they have alligator snouts.

Complete with deadly alligator teeth.

You can barely take your eyes off their reflected images.

"Come on!" Laura snaps you out of it.

But she also attracts the humanigators' attention!

"After them!" a humanigator snarls.

Turn to PAGE 41.

You open the door marked PLAYTIME. How scary could that be? You duck as something whizzes over your head.

"What was that?" you cry.

"It's another of those bouncing balls," Laura explains. She points to a large purple ball bouncing itself around the room.

"Look at all this stuff!" Wendy exclaims, dashing past you. John follows her.

You gaze around the brightly lit room. "Wow," you murmur, staring at the piles of toys. You must be in some kind of playroom.

Then you notice something very strange.

These toys are *all* playing themselves!

Toy cars race around the room. Laura stares at a toy puppet maneuvering its own strings. John chases after another bouncing ball. Wendy giggles at a dancing toy monkey.

You notice a blue top lying at your feet. "Shouldn't this thing be spinning?" You bend down to give it a twirl.

"I don't think you should touch it," Laura warns you.

It's only a top, you think. But maybe Laura is right. Things have a funny way of behaving unexpectedly here.

If you spin the top, turn to PAGE 117.
If you leave it alone, turn to PAGE 33.

132

"Hey," you exclaim, "why are we going underground?"

"Shortcut," the man explains. "We'll come out in my rooms and then the movie theater is right next door."

"Don't worry," Laura assures you. "These weird old houses often have tunnels."

You shrug and keep going. The farther you walk, the darker the tunnel becomes. A terrible smell hangs in the air. Finally the path begins to climb upward again.

The old man reaches overhead. With a loud grunt he shoves open a trapdoor. You all scramble up and out of the tunnel.

Into a crypt!

Turn to PAGE 103.

You sit at the piano. You take a deep breath. You cautiously put your fingers onto the keys — uh, teeth. You play the notes:

D-E-A-D-F-A-C-E

"Aaaahhhhhh!" you shriek as the piano's teeth chomp down on your fingers.

All five doors burst open. Instruments tumble out, attacking Laura and the twins. The piano chews its way up your arm. A tuba swallows Laura. A harp slices through John with its strings. A violin bow saws Wendy in half.

Yep, you should have been paying more attention during your music lessons.

Can you spell

THE END?

You dive underwater. A Jet Ski roars over you.

You burst back up through the surface of the water. "What was that?" you sputter.

"That was Dr. Aqua," a voice behind you says.

You kick hard underwater to turn yourself around. "Agent Z!" you gasp.

Up on the movie screen, Agent Z bobs on a single water ski propelled by a handheld motor. He wears his trademark sunglasses. "Dr. Aqua has escaped into your world," he tells you. "That's never happened before. I need your help."

You stare at the agent. He needs help from *you*?

"But what can we do?" Laura asks.

Agent Z gazes at you. Or at least you think he does. It's hard to tell with those sunglasses.

"You have two choices," he tells you. "You can either try to stop him in your reality. Or you can help me foil his evil scheme in my world. It's up to you."

You heard him.

Decide!

To enter the movie with Agent Z, turn to PAGE 44.

To chase after Dr. Aqua in your world, turn to PAGE 98.

"Let's stick to drier land," you decide.

You and Laura continue on. The brutal heat makes you sweat. Branches smack you in the face. Your skin tingles.

Laura glances at you. "Uh-oh," she comments.

"What is it?" you ask. You scratch your arm.

"You're turning bright red," Laura tells you. "And you're starting to puff up."

You glance down. Laura is right. The itching sensation is horrible! Your flesh feels as if it's crawling with bugs. You wish you could jump out of your skin.

"It must be some kind of allergic reaction," you mumble. Your lips and tongue are swollen, making it hard to speak.

A crackling sound off to the side startles you. You grab Laura's hand and yank her down into a bush.

The hunter appears a moment later.

"I think you need a doctor," Laura whispers. "We should go talk to that guy."

You hate to admit it, but she's right. You're feeling worse by the minute. You have to get the hunter to help you.

Even if it means agreeing to be bait for the giant ape.

Ask the hunter for help on PAGE 65.

You feel around for the humanigator costume. It's a bit big, but you feel much safer wearing it. You leave your wet suit behind and climb out of the vent.

You find yourself in a dimly lit corridor. Monitoring devices line the walls. Strange whooshing sounds echo as machinery regulates the environment. The air is steamy, almost tropical.

You hurry toward what you hope is the main door. You turn a corner — and your heart nearly stops.

Humanigators! Standing guard in front of a room marked LABORATORY.

Agent Z said the main door was in the next corridor over. You're going to have to make it past these guys.

Turn to PAGE 13.

"Aggh!" you scream. You yank off the 3-D glasses. "What's happening to — AAAAAGGHH!"

The huge ape is reaching right out of the screen! Straight toward you!

"That's why the screen went black," you say in horror. "He was so close all we could see was part of him!"

You gasp as the giant ape's enormous fingers curl around you and Laura. He lifts you high into the air.

"He's pulling us into the movie!" Laura shrieks.

She's right! The ape drags you from the dark movie theater into the bright, steamy jungle.

Your heart thuds with terror.

How can this be happening?

Turn to PAGE 122.

About R.L. Stine

R.L. Stine is the most popular author in America. He is the creator of the *Goosebumps, Give Yourself Goosebumps, Fear Street,* and *Ghosts of Fear Street* series, among other popular books. He has written nearly 200 scary novels for kids. Bob lives in New York City with his wife, Jane, teenage son, Matt, and dog, Nadine.

No more clowning around!

GIVE YOURSELF

Special Edition 3: POWER PLAY

Goosebumps®

R.L. STINE

Want to take a ride on the flying trapeze? Become a sideshow freak? Or try on some clown makeup—that won't come off?

Whichever adventure you choose, you'd better take the right POWER objects with you—if you want to make it out of this evil circus alive!

Give Yourself Goosebumps Special #3:

Trapped in the Circus of Fear

Join the circus at a bookstore near you!

Visit the Web site at http://www.scholastic.com/goosebumps